THE Hairy BOOK

To Lucinda Prior-Cowans
the hairiest baby in the world

Other books by Babette Cole

THE Hairy BOOK

Babette Cole

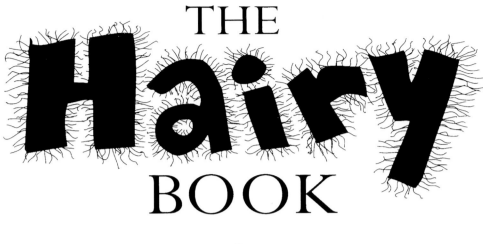

RED FOX

Hair, hair, all kinds of hair,

Hair on your head . . .

and hair elsewhere,

Hair on legs,

hair in a wave...

Hair that you might have to shave.

Hairy hats and hairy feet . . .

Hair that doesn't smell too sweet!

Hair that's red,
Hair that's blue . . .

How many little hairs have you?
I know what will make you laugh . . .

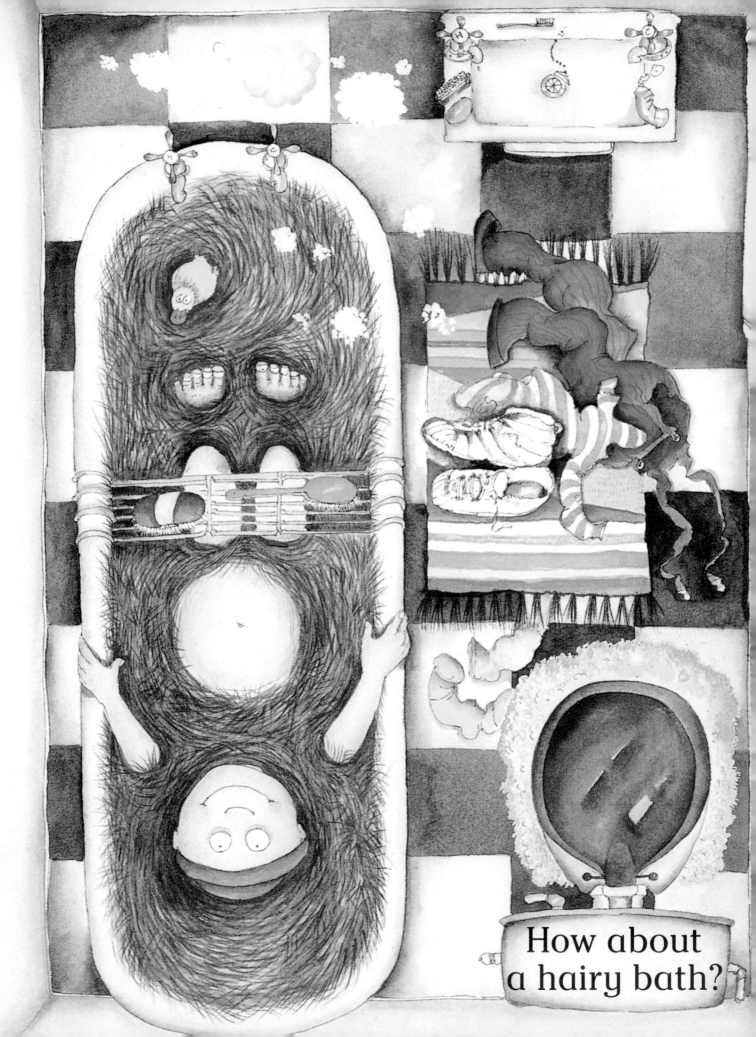

How about a hairy bath?

Hairy coats from hairy goats,

Hairy bogs with hairy frogs . . .

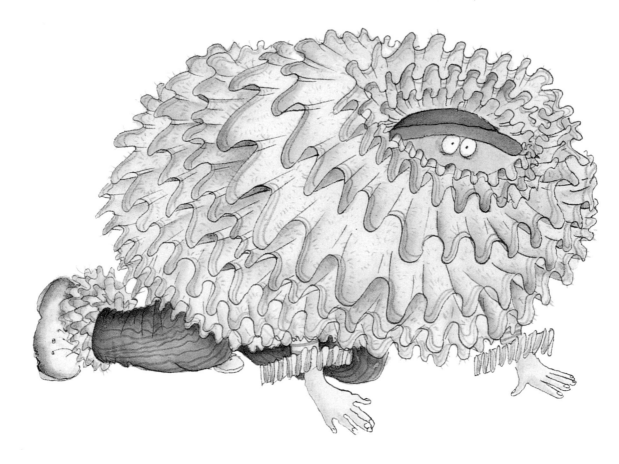

Hairy ruffs and hairy toughs,

Hairy cats and hairy rats
Have little fleas with hairy knees!

What hairy things, do you suppose,
Live up a big fat warty nose?

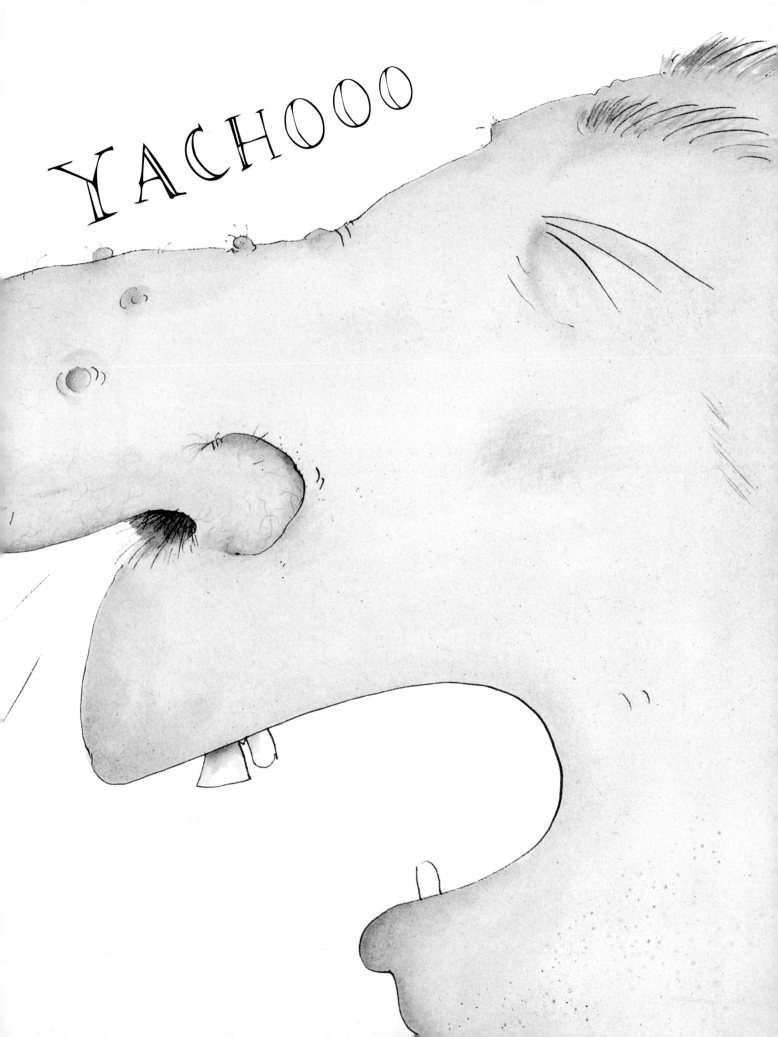

Hairy pants

with hairy ants,

Hairy vests with hairy nests . . .

Have things that hatch

and make me scratch!

Hairy socks

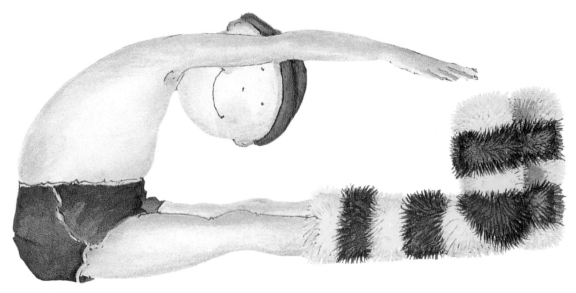

and hairy shirts,

and beefy
Scots with
hairy skirts.

Hairy nice

and hairy
scary . . .

Christmas tree with hairy fairy.

Hairy Mum and hairy Dad
Make me sneeze and wheeze like mad.

Grandad says, a pint of best
makes hair grow upon his chest!

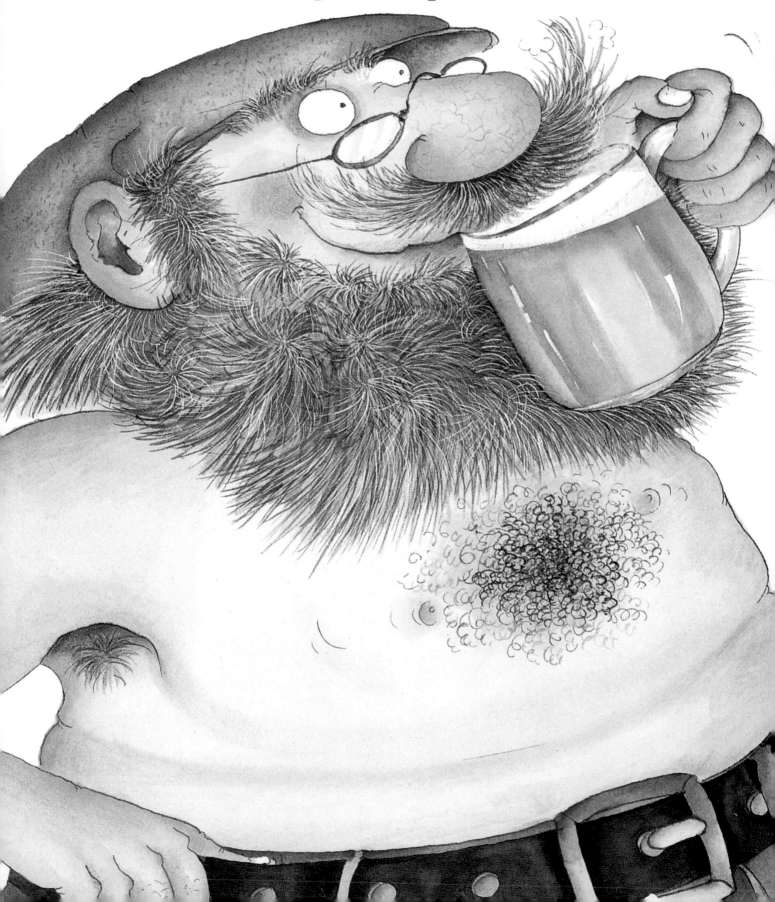

Hairy fruit and hairy bread...

Hairy things beneath the bed,

Hairy big . . .

and hairy small,

I'm glad I have . . .

no hair at all!

THE HAIRY BOOK
A RED FOX BOOK 9781849411141

First published in Great Britain by Jonathan Cape,
an imprint of Random House Children's Books

Jonathan Cape edition published 1984
Red Fox edition published 2003

3 5 7 9 10 8 6 4

Red Fox Books are published by Random House Children's Books,
61–63 Uxbridge Road, London W5 5SA,
a division of The Random House Group Ltd,
in Australia by Random House Australia (Pty) Ltd,
20 Alfred Street, Milsons Point, Sydney, NSW 2061, Australia,
in New Zealand by Random House New Zealand Ltd,
18 Poland Road, Glenfield, Auckland 10, New Zealand,
and in South Africa by Random House (Pty) Ltd,
Endulini, 5A Jubilee Road, Parktown 2193, South Africa

THE RANDOM HOUSE GROUP Limited Reg. No. 954009
www.kidsatrandomhouse.co.uk

A CIP catalogue record for this book is available from the British Library.

Printed in Singapore

More Red Fox picture books
for you to enjoy

ELMER
by David McKee 0099697203

MUMMY LAID AN EGG!
by Babette Cole 0099299119

THE RUNAWAY TRAIN
by Benedict Blathwayt 0099385716

DOGGER
by Shirley Hughes 009992790X

WHERE THE WILD THINGS ARE
by Maurice Sendak 0099408392

OLD BEAR
by Jane Hissey 0099265761

ALFIE GETS IN FIRST
by Shirley Hughes 0099855607

OI! GET OFF OUR TRAIN
by John Burningham 009985340X

GORGEOUS!
by Caroline Castle and Sam Childs 0099400766